Something Old

Ruth Craft and
Nicola Smee

A & C Black · London

Published 1992 by A & C Black (Publishers) Ltd
35 Bedford Row, London WC1R 4JH

Text copyright © 1992 Ruth Craft
Illustrations copyright © 1992 Nicola Smee

Reprinted 1993

ISBN 0–7136–3538–X

A CIP catalogue record for this book
is available from the British Library.

Filmset by Kalligraphic Design Ltd, Horley, Surrey
Printed in Great Britain by William Clowes Ltd, Beccles and London

Chapter One

Mrs Simpson's class were all sitting on the mat listening to a story.

It was about the oldest dinosaur on earth. She lived in the oldest, steamiest swamp in the world which was surrounded by scaly old birds, old gnarled and bent trees and old gigantic toads. She ruled the swamp with a terrible gleam in her small fierce eyes.

Everybody listened quietly.
Everybody except Kevin O'Reilly.
Kevin whispered

and

wriggled.

4

and wriggled

and whispered.

I wonder why Mrs Simpson's teeth look funny when she says 'Sssh!'

Mrs Simpson had to stop the story.

Kevin sat still and pushed his legs
straight out in front of him. His
shoes poked Sharon Thomas in
the back.

6

Kevin sat quietly
and stared at
Mrs Simpson's legs.

Mrs Simpson went
on with the story . . .

The Queen of the Dinosaurs was
fifty metres long and had teeth
as big as a man's hand.

She defended her swamp against
any invader until she got very
old and tired.

'Oh, I wish I was young again,' said the
old Queen Dinosaur, and she cried a
bit and made the swamp even
wetter and
steamier.

But then she saw all the dinosaurs in the world coming through the steaming forest, including

Brontosaurus

Stegosaurus

Many happy returns!

And they carried between them a huge green leafy cake with 200 candles flickering in the gloom of the steamy swamp

'TERRIFIC!' roared the Queen of the Dinosaurs. 'You've remembered my BIRTHDAY!' And she cheered up right away, blowing out all her candles with one enormous puff that knocked down a few trees as well.

Then she shared out her leafy green cake with all the dinosaurs in the world.

Mrs Simpson closed the story book.

'Now, tomorrow,' said Mrs Simpson, 'we are all going to start work on our new project. It's going to be about the olden days and olden things. I'm going to give you a note to take home.'

'Ask your parents if you can bring
to school any interesting old things
that you can find around the house.

You might be able to find an old
biscuit tin,

or some
old clothes,

or a
letter or

photograph.

Some things that are very old are
very precious so we shall have to be
very careful.'

Kevin thought that
Mrs Simpson's legs
looked pretty old,
but he didn't say
anything.

They look pretty old to me!

Chapter Two

Kevin O'Reilly lost his note and he forgot to tell his mum about the new project because he was very busy helping her fix the light in the bathroom.

Kevin handed his mum the screwdriver and held the torch.

Can you see Mum?

Move it this way a bit, love.

When the lights came on, Kevin and his mum had their supper in front of the telly.

Then they played a game that they had invented. It was called Rhubarb Whist and the person who got three aces and three kings in their hand had to bang the table hard and shout 'Rhubarb!'

Rhubarb! Rhubarb!

And Rhubarb to you, mate!

When Kevin went to sleep he had an interesting dream about the Queen of the Dinosaurs who turned out to be very good at fixing things. She also knew some good jokes.

In the morning, Kevin remembered about the project. He asked his mum if she had anything old he could take to school but she didn't quite understand.

Here you are. Have this old stamp. It's been in my purse for ages. It's all grotty and old!

Kevin took the
stamp to school.

Chapter Three

Mrs Simpson asked everybody what they had brought to school.

Sharon Thomas had brought a beautiful old lace shawl with a note from her mum.

The note said,

'Oooh! Aaah!' said all the children.
'It must be very old.'

'Oooh! Aaah!' said Mrs Simpson.
'How beautiful. We must look after
it very carefully.'

The other children had brought old shoes, old photograph albums and even an old football jersey.

Justine Jones brought a picture of
her mum when she was a baby.

'Oooh! Aaah!' said all the children.

'Oooh! Aaah!' said Mrs Simpson.
'Look children! Isn't she a pretty
baby? And don't you think she looks
just a little bit like Justine?'

'Oooh! Aaah!' said all the children.
'Oooh! Aaah!' said Mrs Simpson.

'Yuk,' said Kevin O'Reilly.

And now Kevin dear, what have you brought to show us?

Kevin dug in his pocket. He found the old crinkly, wrinkly stamp.

He tried to smooth it out with his thumb.

30

'It's a stamp,' he said. 'It's been in my mum's purse for ages.'

That's a tatty old stamp.

Doesn't look very precious to me!

Yes well, that's very nice. Thank you Kevin.

'Please Miss! Please Miss!' said Desmond Dowson. 'I've got some stamps too.'

And Desmond showed the
class a beautiful old red
book, filled with stamps
from lots of different
countries.

There were stamps
of kings and queens

stamps of
flowers and
mountains

33

'These stamps belonged to my uncle but my auntie said I could have them,' said Desmond Dowson. 'My mum said if I was very careful, I could bring them to school.'

'Oh yes!' said Mrs Simpson. 'We'll be very careful. Thank you very much, Desmond, for thinking of the very thing that we wanted for our project.'

Desmond Dowson smiled.

Kevin felt rotten.

At break, Kevin sat by himself. He watched Justine Jones, Sharon Thomas and Desmond Dowson skipping.

Rosy Apple, Lemon Tart, tell me the name of your sweetheart.
All the boys in our town live a happy life except for Desmond who is looking for a wife . . . .

Kevin went off to play football and kicked the goal post as hard as he could.

Chapter Four

Kevin and his mum had meatballs
and macaroni for supper.

Kevin grated the cheese

and watched the meatballs

while his mum paid the bills.

She paid the electric and the gas,
then the phone and then she said,
'You haven't still got that stamp I
gave you this morning, have you?'

Kevin explained that he'd left it at
school.

Over supper, Kevin was a bit quiet.

Kevin's mum said, 'Tell me.'

And Kevin did.

He told his mum all about the
dinosaur story.

He told her all about
the project

and Sharon Thomas

and Justine Jones.

He told her about how rotten he felt
when he only had one grotty old
stamp and he told her all about
Desmond Dowson and the beautiful
red book of stamps.

They were beautiful stamps mum and they were very precious. There was one like a lovely rose that was ever so old.

'Everybody's got something old and precious in their family – except me,' Kevin complained. 'I've got nothing old and precious. I've got no lace shawls or pictures of you when you were a baby or books of stamps.

All I've got is my old trainers. And they're not very old or precious.'

Kevin's mum looked upset. But then she got up and sat next to Kevin and put her arms around him.

'Listen, Kevin. You *have* got something old and precious and valuable. Think about it. Think hard. I'll put the kettle on and we'll make a plan.'

Chapter Five

A week later the project was finished.

Mrs Simpson sent a special note home to ask all the parents and families to come and see it.

It was all arranged in one corner of the classroom. There were posters saying, 'These are the stamps that belonged to Desmond's uncle' and 'Here is a picture of Justine's mum when she was a baby' and 'Here is Sharon's grandmother's shawl'.

And as well as that there were old
letters,

old photographs,

old biscuit and tea and coffee tins,

pictures of
old dogs and cats,

baby boots and baby bonnets and
old cups and saucers and plates.

The Head Teacher came in to see the project and to welcome the parents and the families. The room was very crowded and hot.

Everybody was talking about the project. Nobody noticed that Kevin O'Reilly wasn't there.

Suddenly the door opened.

In came Kevin O'Reilly with a very old lady. She walked slowly . . .

. . . and she needed two sticks and Kevin's arm to help her.

Kevin carried her big black handbag
and carefully helped her towards
the project.

Everybody was silent.

Kevin made the old lady comfortable in a chair and then he said, 'This is my Great Grandmother O'Reilly. She is ninety-nine years old. She is the mother of my grandmother and she was born in Ireland.

She is the oldest and most valuable
person we have got in our family
and I have brought her to
the project.'

Great Grandmother O'Reilly was older than anything else in the whole room!

The lady from the Town Hall came over to shake her hand

and the man from the newspaper took her picture.

Great Grandmother O'Reilly smiled
and winked at all the children and
Mrs Simpson made her a cup of tea.

She was so busy laughing and
joking that she hardly had time to
drink it.

'Listen,' said Great Grandmother O'Reilly. 'Did you hear about the dad who gave his little boy 10p and a pat on the head every time he was good. What do you think he had by the time he was ten?'

Everybody laughed and Great
Grandmother O'Reilly told
them about her school
when she was little.

She told them about all the games
they played and she asked the
children to sing and show her some
of their games.

Justine Jones and Sharon Thomas
sang 'Rosy Apple, Lemon Tart' and
Great Grandmother O'Reilly joined
in. 'I know this one,' she said.

Everybody joined in. Desmond Dowson even climbed up on the biggest chair so that everybody could see and hear him.

Kevin felt proud of his great grandmother. He thought about the Queen of the Dinosaurs and wondered if his gran ever felt lonely and forgotten. She didn't look lonely or forgotten now as she sat there singing her head off.

'Tell that silly little boy there not to show off so much,' she said pointing to Desmond Dowson.

Kevin grinned.

He'd been wanting to say that to Desmond Dowson for ages.